DIANE SIEBERT

MOJAVE

PAINTINGS BY WENDELL MINOR

Thomas Y. Crowell • New York

Mojave
Text copyright © 1988 by Diane Siebert
Illustrations copyright © 1988 by Wendell Minor
Printed in the U.S.A. All rights reserved.

Library of Congress Cataloging-in-Publication Data
Siebert, Diane.
  Mojave.

  Summary: Evokes the land and animals of the Mojave
Desert in poetic text and illustrations.
    1. Mojave Desert (Calif.)—Juvenile poetry.
[1. Mojave Desert (Calif.)—Poetry. 2. Deserts—
Poetry. 3. American poetry] I. Minor, Wendell, ill.
II. Title.
PS3569.I36M6 1988   811'.54 [E]   86-24329
ISBN 0-690-04567-0
ISBN 0-690-04569-7 (lib. bdg.)

        1 2 3 4 5 6 7 8 9 10
             First Edition

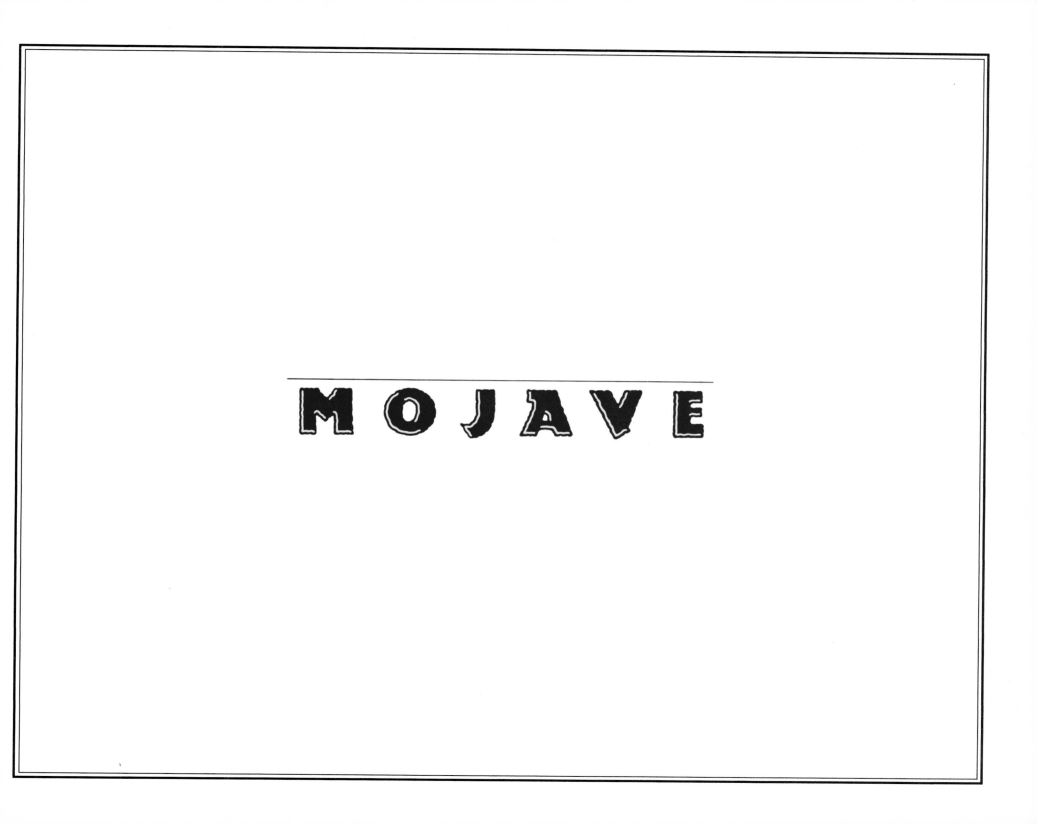

MOJAVE

I am the desert.
I am free.
Come walk the sweeping face of me.

Through canyon eyes of sandstone red
I see the hawk, his wings outspread;
He sunward soars to block the light
And casts the shadow of his flight
Upon my vast and ancient face,
Whose deep arroyos boldly trace
The paths where sudden waters run—
Long streams of tears dried by the sun.

I feel the windstorm's violent thrust;
I feel the sting of sand and dust
As bit by bit, and year by year,
New features on my face appear.

Great mountain ranges stretch for miles
To crease my face with frowns and smiles.
My lakes are dry and marked by tracks
Of zigging, zagging, long-eared jacks.
Dust devils swirl and slowly rise;
They whistle, whirling to the skies,
While tossed and blown in great stampedes
Are stumbling, bumbling tumbleweeds.

I feel the tread of tiny feet
As lizards dart in swift retreat
To hide in shadows, safe, unseen,
Beneath the yucca's spears of green.
Here Joshua trees, in mighty stands,
Spread twisted arms and sharp, green hands
Above the tortoises who sleep
Within the shade, then slowly creep
Across my rocks, in armored domes,
To crawl inside their burrowed homes;
And snakes with lovely, patterned skin
Go gliding, hiding deep within
My rocky face, far from the light,
Protected, cool, and out of sight.

Above, I hear a raucous cry
And see the bold, black raven fly
On waves of wind, to make his way
Across the endless stretch of day.
And just as far as he can see,
Creosote bushes cover me;
From limestone cliffs to white salt flats,
They shelter insects, birds, and rats.

Here, silvery mirages dance
Among the prickly cactus plants
Whose spines and bristles help them thrive
Where weaker plants could not survive.
The beavertails; the hedgehogs stout;
The jointed chollas reaching out;
The barrel cacti, fat and round—
All live upon my arid ground.

High on a ridge wild mustangs stand;
They stare across the sunbaked land,
And sensing danger, turn in fear
To gallop off and disappear.

Within my valleys, ghost towns lie;
Their crumbling walls personify
The dreams of those who used to be—
Of those who tried to conquer me.

Here, long ago, the miners came
To seek their fortunes and their fame—
To find the silver and the gold
That deep inside myself I hold.
They came to me with lofty hopes
And left behind, upon my slopes,
Their burros, whose descendants roam
On this, their harsh adopted home.

And as the desert seasons change,
The hands of Nature rearrange
My timeworn face with new designs
Of colors, shadows, shapes, and lines:

In wintertime the north winds blow;
My mountain peaks are capped with snow;
But resting, waiting patiently
Beneath the frost that covers me,
I dream of spring, when I can wear
The blossoms of the prickly pear,
Along with flowers, wild and bright,
And butterflies in joyful flight.

My summer face is cracked and dry,
All blotched and flecked with alkali,
Until the coming of a storm
When thunderclouds above me form,
And bursting, send their rains to pound
Across my high, unyielding ground
Where walls of water grow, and flow
Toward my valleys far below.

But soon the blazing sun breaks through,
And then, beneath skies wide and blue,
My features shimmer, blurred by heat,
Till autumn breezes, cool and sweet,
Caress my face, now brown and burned,
To tell me autumn has returned,
To touch the land where coyotes prowl,
Where coyotes lift their heads and howl;
At night they sing their songs to me:

We are the desert.
We are free.

And on my mountains, craggy, steep,
I feel the hooves of bighorn sheep;
From shelf to rocky shelf they spring,
Their hoofbeats
                echo...
                      echoing....

I am the desert.
Feel the breeze
That dances through the Joshua trees.

I am the desert.
Hear me cry
With raven voices in the sky.

I am the desert.
I am free.
Come walk the sweeping face of me.

DIANE SIEBERT lives with her husband in White Pine County, Nevada, north of the vast Mojave Desert, an area that covers thousands of square miles of southern California, southern Nevada, and small portions of Utah and Arizona. Her love for the land is a continuing source of inspiration for her writing. She and her husband have traveled extensively through most of the United States and Mexico, and it was those years of travel that prompted her to write her first book, TRUCK SONG.

WENDELL MINOR was graduated from the Ringling School of Art and Design in Sarasota, Florida, and later spent several summers painting in the Southwest. He is the recipient of over 200 professional awards, including awards from the Society of Illustrators, American Illustration Annual, and Graphis Annual, and is currently the executive vice president of the Society of Illustrators. A teacher for twelve years at the School of Visual Arts in New York, he is well known in the publishing industry for the paintings he has done for the jackets of many best-selling novels.